My Shipm

Columbus

Stephen Marlowe

Alpha Editions

This edition published in 2024

ISBN : 9789361470219

Design and Setting By
Alpha Editions
www.alphaedis.com
Email - info@alphaedis.com

MY SHIPMATE—COLUMBUS
By STEPHEN WILDER

We've been taught from childhood that the earth is round and that Columbus discovered America. But maybe we take too much on faith. This first crossing for instance. Were you there? Did you see Columbus land? Here's the story of a man who can give us the straight facts.

THE laughter brought spots of color to his cheeks. He stood there for a while, taking it, and then decided he had had enough and would sit down. A whisper of amusement still stirred the room as he returned to his seat and the professor said,

"But just a moment, Mr. Jones. Won't you tell the class what makes you think Columbus was not the 'bold skipper' the history books say he was. After all, Mr. Jones, this is a history class. If you know more or better history than the history books do, isn't it your duty to tell us?"

He clutched at his slashed veins and snarled into the face of death.

"I didn't say he *wasn't*," Danny Jones said desperately as the laughter started again. Some profs were like that, he thought. Picking on one student and making the rest of the class laugh and think what a great guy the prof was and what a prize dodo the hapless student was. "I said," Danny went on doggedly, "Columbus might not have been—maybe wasn't—the bold skipper the history books claim he was. I can't prove it. No one can. I haven't a time machine."

Again it was the wrong thing to say. The professor wagged a finger in front of his face and gave Danny a sly look. "Don't you," he said, "don't you indeed? I was beginning to think you had been willed H. G. Wells' famous literary invention, young man." That one had the class all but rolling in the aisles.

Danny said desperately, "No! No, I mean, they don't even know for sure if Columbus was born in Genoa. They just think he was. So they also could be wrong about—"

Abruptly the professor's face went serious. "My dear Mr. Jones," he said slowly, acidly, "don't you think we've had enough of fantasy? Don't you think we ought to return to history?"

Danny sat down and for a moment shut his eyes but remained conscious of everyone looking at him, staring at him, evaluating. It wasn't so easy, he decided, being a sophomore transfer student from a big city college, where almost everything went and there was a certain amount of anonymity in the very size of the classes, to a small town college where every face, after a week or so, was familiar. Danny wished he had kept his big yap shut about Columbus, but it was too late now. They'd be ribbing him for weeks....

On his way back to the dorm after classes he was hailed by a student who lived down the hall from him, a fellow named Groves, who said, "How's the boy, Danny. Next thing you'll tell us is that Cortez was really a sexy Spanish broad with a thirty-eight bust who conquered Montezuma and his Indians with sex appeal. Get it, boy. I said—"

"Aw, lay off," Danny grumbled.

The other boy laughed, then shrugged, then said, "Oh yeah, forgot to tell you. There's a telegram waiting for you in the dorm. House-mother's got it. Well, see you, Vasco da Gama."

Danny trudged on to the Georgian-style dormitory and went inside, through the lobby and behind the stairs to the house-mother's office at the rear of the building. She was a kindly-looking old woman with a halo of white hair and a smile which made her a good copy of everyone's grandmother. But now her face was set in unexpectedly grim lines. "Telegram for you, Danny," she said slowly. "They read it over the telephone first, then delivered it." She held out a yellow envelope. "I'm afraid it's some bad news, Danny." She seemed somehow reluctant to part with the little yellow envelope.

"What is it?" Danny said.

"You'd better read it yourself. Here, sit down."

Danny nodded, took the envelope, sat down and opened it. He read, MR. DANNY JONES, WHITNEY COLLEGE, WHITNEY, VIRGINIA. REGRET TO INFORM YOU UNCLE AVERILL PASSED AWAY LAST NIGHT PEACEFULLY IN HIS SLEEP LEAVING UNSPECIFIED PROPERTY TO YOU. It was signed with a name Danny did not recognize.

"I'm terribly sorry," the house-mother said, placing her hand on Danny's shoulder.

"Oh, that's all right, Mrs. Grange. It's all right. You see, Uncle Averill wasn't a young man. He must have been in his eighties."

"Were you very close to him, Danny?"

"No, not for a long time. When I was a kid—"

Mrs. Grange smiled.

"Well, when I was eight or nine, I used to see him all the time. We stayed at his place on the coast near St. Augustine, Florida, for a year. I—I feel sorry about Uncle Averill, Mrs. Grange, but I feel better about something that happened in class today. I—I think Uncle Averill would have approved of how I acted."

"Want to talk about it?"

"Well, it's just he always said never to take any so-called fact for granted, especially in history. I can almost remember his voice now, the way he used to say, 'if ever there's an argument in history, sonny, all you ever get is the propaganda report of the side which won.' You know, Mrs. Grange, I think he was right. Of course, a lot of folks thought old Uncle Averill was a little queer. Touched in the head is what they said."

"They oughtn't to say such things."

"Always tinkering around in his basement. Funny, nobody ever knew on what. He wouldn't let anybody near the place. He had a time lock and everything. What nobody could figure out is if he was trying so hard to guard something that was in the basement, why did he sometimes disappear for weeks on end without even telling anybody where he went. And I remember," Danny went on musing, "every time he came back he went into that harangue about history, as if somehow he had confirmed his suspicions. He was a funny old guy but I liked him."

"You remembering him so vividly after all these years will be the best epitaph your uncle could have, Danny. But what are you going to do? About what he left you, I mean."

"Uncle Averill always liked promptness. If he left something for me, he'd want me to pick it up immediately. I guess I ought to go down there to St. Augustine as fast as I can."

"But your classes—"

"I'll have to take an emergency leave of absence."

"Under the circumstances, I'm sure the college will approve. Do you think your uncle left you anything—well—important?"

"Important?" Danny repeated the word. "No, I don't think so. Not by the world's standards. But it must have been important to Uncle Averill. He was a—you know, an image-breaker—"

"An iconoclast," supplied Mrs. Grange.

"Yes'm, an iconoclast. But I liked him."

Mrs. Grange nodded. "You'd better get over and see the Dean."

An hour later, Danny was at the bus depot, waiting for the Greyhound that would take him over to Richmond, where he would meet a train for the south and Florida.

It was a rambling white stucco house with a red tile roof and a pleasant grove of palm trees in front and flame-red hibiscus climbing the stucco. The lawyer, whose name was Tartalion, met him at the door.

"I'll get right down to business, Mr. Jones," Tartalion said after they had entered the house. "Your uncle wanted it that way."

"Wait a minute," Danny said, "don't tell me they already had the funeral?"

"Your uncle didn't believe in funerals. His will stipulated cremation."

"But, it was so—"

"Sudden? I know, the will wasn't officially probated. But your uncle had a judge for a friend, and under the circumstances, his wishes were granted. Now, then, you know why you're here?"

"You mean, what he left me? I thought I'd at least get to see his—"

"His body? Not your uncle, not old Averill Jones. You ought to know better. Sonny," the lawyer asked abruptly, "how well did you know the old man?"

The sonny rankled. After all, Danny thought, I'm nineteen. I like beer and girls and I'm no sonny anymore. He sighed and thought of his history class, then thought of Uncle Averill's opinion of history, and felt better. He explained the relationship to Mr. Tartalion and waited for the lawyer to speak.

"Well, it beats me," Tartalion admitted. "Why he left it to a nephew he hasn't seen in ten or eleven years, I mean. Don't just look at me like that. You know that contraption he had in the basement, don't you? How he wouldn't let a soul near it, ever? Then tell me something, Danny. Why did he leave it to you?"

"You're joking!" Danny cried.

"I was your uncle's lawyer. I wouldn't joke about it. He said it was the only thing he had worth willing. He said he willed it to you. Want me to read you the clause?"

Danny nodded. He felt strangely flattered, because the contraption in Averill Jones' basement—a contraption which no one but Averill Jones had ever seen—had been the dearest thing in the old bachelor's life. Actually, he was not Danny's uncle, but his grand-uncle. He had lived alone in St. Augustine and had liked living alone. The only relative he had tolerated was Danny, when Danny was a small boy. Then, as Danny approached his ninth birthday, the old man had said, "They're teaching you too much at school, son. Too many wrong things, too many highfalutin' notions, too much just plain old hogwash. Why don't you kind of make yourself scarce for a few years?" It had been blunt and to the point. It had made Danny cry. He hadn't thought of what had happened that last day he'd seen his grand-uncle for years, but he thought of it now.

"But why can't I come back and see you?" he had asked tearfully.

"On account of the machine, son."

"But *why*, uncle?"

"Hey, come on now and stop your blubbering all over me. If you can't you can't."

"You have to tell me why!"

"Stubborn little critter. Well, I like that. All right, I'll tell you why. Because the machine has a funny kind of fuel, that's why. It doesn't run on gasoline, Danny, or anything like that."

"What does it do, uncle?"

But the old man had shaken his head. "Maybe someday after I'm gone you'll find out. If anyone finds out, it will be you, and that's a promise."

"You still didn't tell me why I have to go away."

"Because—well, don't go telling this to your folks, son, or they'll think old Uncle Averill has a screw loose somewheres—because that machine I have downstairs runs on faith. On faith, you understand? Oh, not the kind of faith they think is important and do a lot of talking and sermoning about, but a different kind of faith. Personal faith, you might say. Faith in a dream or a belief, no matter what people think. And—you know what ruins that faith?"

"No," Danny had said, his eyes very big.

"Knowledge!" cried his uncle. "Too much so-called knowledge which isn't knowledge at all, but hearsay. That's what they're teaching you. In school, other places, every day of your life. I'll tell you when you can come back, Danny: when you're ready to throw most of it overboard. All right?"

He had had to say all right. It was the last time he had ever seen his uncle, but those weren't the last words Averill Jones had spoken to him, for the old man had added as he got up to go: "Don't forget, son. Don't let them pull the wool over your eyes. History is propaganda—from a winner's point of view. If a side lost the war and got stamped on, you never see the war from its point of view. If an idea got out of favor and stamped on, the idea is ridiculed. Don't forget it, son. If you believe something, if you *know* it's right, have faith in it and don't give a mind what people say. Promise?"

Danny, his eyes stinging with tears because somehow he could sense he would never see Uncle Averill again, had said that he promised.

"... to my nephew, Danny Jones," the lawyer was reading. "So, you see, you'll have to go right down there and look the thing over. Naturally, I'll have to leave the house while you do so and I won't be able to return until you tell me I can—"

"But why?"

"Weren't you listening?"

"I guess I was thinking about my uncle."

"Well, the clause says you're to examine the machine alone, with no one else in the house. It's perfectly legal. If that's what your uncle wanted, that's what he'll get. Are you all set?"

Danny nodded and Tartalion shook his hand solemnly, then left the room. Danny heard the lawyer's footsteps receding, heard the front door open and close, heard a car engine start. Then, slowly, he walked through the living room of his dead uncle's house and across the long, narrow kitchen and to the basement stairs. His hands were very dry and he felt his heart thudding. He was nervous, which surprised him.

But why? he thought, why should it surprise me? All my life, Uncle Averill's basement has been a mystery. Let's face it, Danny-boy, you haven't exactly had an adventurous life. Maybe Uncle Averill was the biggest adventure in it, with his secret machine and strange disappearances. And maybe Uncle Averill did a good selling job when you were small, because that machine means mystery to you. It's probably not much more than a better mousetrap, but you want to believe it is, don't you? And you're nervous because the way Uncle Averill kept you and anyone else away from his basement when you were a kid makes it a kind of frightening place, even now.

He opened the basement door with a key which the lawyer had given him. Beyond the door were five steps and another door—this one of metal. It had had a time lock in the old days, Danny remembered, but the lock was gone now. The metal door swung ponderously, like the door to a bank vault, and then Danny was on the other side. It was dark down there, but faint light seeped in through small high windows and in a few moments Danny's eyes grew accustomed to the gloom.

The basement was empty except for what looked like a big old steamer trunk in the center of the dusty cement floor.

Danny was disappointed. He had childhood visions of an intricate maze of machinery cluttering up every available square foot of basement space, but now he knew that whatever it was which had taken up so much of Uncle Averill's time could fit in the odd-looking steamer trunk in the center of the floor and thus wasn't too much bigger than a good-size TV set. He walked slowly to the trunk and stood for a few moments over the lid. It was an ancient-looking steamer: Uncle Averill must have owned it since his own youth. Still, just a plain trunk.

Danny was in no hurry to open the lid, which did not seem to be locked. For a few moments, at least, he could shield himself from further disappointment—because now he had a hunch that Uncle Averill's machine was going to be a first-class dud. Maybe, he thought gloomily, Uncle Averill had simply not liked to be with people and had used the ruse of a bank-vault door and an empty steamer trunk to achieve privacy whenever he felt the need for it.

Remembering the history class, Danny decided that—after all—sometimes that wasn't a bad idea. Finally, he called himself a fool for waiting and threw up the trunk-lid.

A small case was all he saw inside, although the interior of the trunk was larger than he had expected. A man could probably curl up in there quite comfortably. But the case—the case looked exactly like it ought to house a tape-recorder.

Danny reached in and hauled out the case. It was heavy, about as heavy as a tape-recorder ought to be. Danny placed it down on the floor and opened it.

What he saw was a battery-powered tape-recorder. His disappointment increased: Uncle Averill had left a message for him, that was all. Dutifully, however, he set the spools and snapped on the switch.

A voice from yesterday—Uncle Averill's voice—spoke to him.

"Hallo, Danny," it said. "The way the years roll by, I forget exactly how old you are, boy. Seventeen? Eighteen? Twenty? Well, it doesn't matter—if you still believe. If you have faith. Faith in what? Maybe now you're old enough to know. I mean faith in—not having faith. That is, faith in not taking faithfully all the silly items of knowledge they try to cram down your throat in school. See what I mean? Remember what I always said about history, Danny: you get propaganda, is all, from the winning side. If you got faith enough in yourself, Danny, faith enough not to believe everything the history books tell you, that's the kind of faith I mean. Because such a faith gave me the most interesting life a man ever lived, make no mistake about that.

"I'm dead, Danny. Yep, old Uncle Averill is dead. Because this tape-recorder won't be left you in my will until I am dead. But, no regrets, boy. I had a great life. How great—nobody knows. Only you, you're about to find out. Do you believe? Do you believe the way I have in mind? Make no mistake about it now, son. If you don't believe, you might as well burn these spools and go home."

Danny considered. He remembered what had happened in his history class. Wasn't that the sort of faith Uncle Averill had in mind? Faith not to believe in historical fairy tales? Faith to doubt when one ought to doubt? Faith to be skeptical....

"Good," said the voice from the past. "Then you're still here. Look in front of you, Danny-boy. The trunk. The old steamer. Know what it is?"

"No," Danny said, then clamped a hand over his mouth. For a moment he had actually believed he was talking to the dead man.

"It's a time machine," said his Uncle's voice.

There was a silence. The tape went on winding. For a moment, Danny thought that was all. Then the voice continued: "No, your old grand-uncle isn't nuts, Danny. It's a time machine. I know it's a time machine because I used it all my life. You expected some kind of complicated gadget down here, I know. I made everybody think it was a gadget. Going down to your basement and tinkering with a gadget is fine in our culture. Hell's fire, boy, it's approved behavior. But locking a bank-vault door behind you and curling up in a steamer trunk, that isn't approved. Now, is it?

"I'll tell you about this here time machine, sonny. It isn't a machine at all, in the strict sense of the word. You can see that. It's just—well, an empty box. But it works, and what else ought a fellow to care about.

"Funny how I got it. I was eighteen or twenty, maybe. And my Grand-uncle Daniel gave it to me. Daniel, get me. Daniel to Averill to Daniel. So when you have a grand-nephew, see that his name's Averill, understand? Keep it going, Danny. Because this trunk is old. A lot older than you think.

"And you can travel through time in it. Don't look at me like that, I know what you're thinking. There isn't any such thing as time travel. In the strict sense of the word, it's impossible. You can't resurrect the past or peek into the unborn future. Well, I don't know about the future, but I do know about the past. But you got to have faith, you got to be a kid at heart, Danny. You got to have this dream, see?

"Because you don't travel anywhere. But your mind does, and it's like you wake up in somebody else's body, drawn to him like a magnet, somebody else—some*when* else. Your body stays right here, you see. In the trunk. In what they called suspended animation. But you—the real you, the you that knows how to dream and to believe—you go back.

"Don't make the mistake I made at first. It's no dream in the usual sense of the word. It's real, Danny. You're somebody else back there, all right, but if he gets hurt, you get hurt. If he dies—taps for Danny Jones! You get me?"

The dead man's voice chuckled. "But don't think this means automatically you'll be able to travel through time. Because you got to have the proper attitude. You've got to believe in yourself, and not in all the historical fictions they give you. Now do you understand? If you're skeptical enough and if at the same time you like to dream enough—that's all it takes. Want to try it?"

Suddenly the voice was gone. That was all there was and at first Danny could not believe it. A sense of bitter disappointment enveloped him—not because Uncle Averill had left him nothing but an old steamer trunk but because Uncle Averill had been, to say the least, off his rocker.

The fabulous machine in the basement was—nothing.

Just a steamer trunk and an incredible story about time-traveling.

Danny sighed and began to walk back toward the cellar stairs. He paused. He turned around uncertainly and looked at the trunk. After all, he had promised; at least he'd promised himself that he'd carry out his peculiar uncle's wishes. Besides, he'd come all the way down here from Whitney College and he ought to at least try the machine.

But there wasn't any machine.

Try the trunk then? There was nothing to try except curling up in it and maybe closing the lid. Uncle Averill was a practical joker, too. It might be just like Uncle Averill to have the lid snap shut and lock automatically so Danny would have to pound his knuckles black and blue until the lawyer heard and came for him.

You see, sonny? would be Uncle Averill's point. You believed me, and you should have known better.

Danny cursed himself and returned to the trunk. He gazed down at the yawning interior for a few seconds, then put first one foot, then the other over the side. He sat down and stared at a peeling blue-paper liner. He rolled over and curled up. The bottom of the trunk was a good fit. He reached up and found a rope dangling down toward him. He pulled the lid down, smiling at his own credulity, and was engulfed in total darkness.

But it would be wonderful, he found himself thinking. It would be the most wonderful thing in the world, to be able to travel through time and see for yourself what really had happened in all the world's colorful ages and to take part in the wildest, proudest adventures of mankind.

He thought, I want to believe. It would be so wonderful to believe.

He also thought about his history class. He did not know it, but his history class was very important. It was crucial. Everything depended on his history class. Because he doubted. He did not want to take Columbus' bravery and intelligence for granted. There were no surviving documents, so why should he?

Maybe Columbus was a third-rater!

Maybe—at least you didn't have to worship him as a hero just because he happened to discover ...

Now, what did he discover?

In absolute darkness and a ringing in the ears and far away a dim glowing light and larger and brighter and the whirling whirling spinning flashing I don't believe but strangely somehow I have faith, faith in myself, buzzing, humming, glowing ...

The world exploded.

There was a great deal of laughter in the tavern.

At first he thought the laughter was directed at him. Giddily, he raised his head. He saw raw wood rafters, a leaded glass window, a stained and greasy wall, heavy wood-plank tables with heavy chairs and a barbarous-looking crew drinking from heavy clay mugs. One of the mugs was in front of him and he raised it to his lips without thinking.

It was ale, the strongest ale he had ever tasted. He got it down somehow without gagging. The laughter came again, rolling over him like a wave. A serving girl scurried by, skirts flashing, a rough tray of clay mugs balanced expertly on one hand. A man with a sword dangling at his side staggered to his feet drunkenly and clawed at the girl, but she shoved him back into his seat and kept walking.

The third wave of laughter rolled and then there was a brief silence.

"Drink too much, Martin Pinzon?" Danny's companion at the long board-table asked. He was an evil-looking old man with a patch over one eye and a small white spade-shaped beard and unshaven cheeks.

"Not me," Danny said, amazed because the language was unfamiliar to him yet he could both understand and speak it. "What's so funny?" he asked. "Why's everyone laughing?"

The old man's hand slapped his back and the mouth parted to show ugly blackened teeth and the old man laughed so hard spittle spotted his beard. "As if you didn't know," he managed to say. "As if you didn't know, Martin Pinzon. It's that weak-minded sailor again, the one who claims to have a charter for three caravels from the Queen herself. Drunk as Bacchus and there's his pretty little daughter trying to get him to come home again. I tell you, Martin Pinzon, if he isn't ..."

But now Danny wasn't listening. He looked around the tavern until he saw the butt of all the laughter. Slowly, drawn irresistibly, Martin Pinzon—or Danny Jones—got up and walked over there.

The man was drunk as Bacchus, all right. He was a man perhaps somewhat taller than average. He had a large head with an arrogant beak of a nose dominating the face, but the mouth was weak and irresolute. He stared drunkenly at a beautiful girl who could not have been more than seventeen.

The girl was saying, "Please, papa. Come back to the hotel with me. Papa, don't you realize you're sailing tomorrow?"

"Gowananlemebe," the man mumbled.

"Papa. Please. The Queen's charter—"

"I was drunk when I took it and drunk when I examined those three stinking caravels and—" he leaned forward as if to speak in deepest confidence, but his drunken voice was still very loud—"and drunk when I said the world was round. I—"

"You hear that?" someone cried. "Old Chris was drunk when he said the world was round!"

"He must a' been!" someone else shouted. Everyone laughed.

"Come on, papa," the girl pleaded. She wore a shawl over her dress and another shawl on her head. Her blonde hair barely peeked out, and she was beautiful. She tried to drag her father to his feet by one arm, but he was too heavy for her.

She looked around the room defiantly as the laughter surged again. "Brave men!" she mocked. "A bunch of stay-at-homes. Won't somebody help me? Papa sails tomorrow."

"Papa sails tomorrow," said someone, miming her desperate tones. "Didn't you know that papa sails tomorrow?"

"Not sailing anyplace at all," the father mumbled. "World isn't round. Drunk. Think I want to fall over the edge? Think I—"

"Oh, papa," moaned the girl. "Won't someone help me to—" And she tugged again at the man's arm—"to get him to bed."

A big man nearby boomed, "I'll help you t'bed, me lass, but it won't be with your old father. Eh, mates?" he cried, and the tavern echoed with laughter. The big man got up and went over to the girl. "Now, listen, lass," he said, taking hold of her arm. "Why don't you forget this drunken slob of a father and—"

Crack! Her hand blurred at his cheek, struck it like a pistol shot. The big man blinked his eyes and grinned. "So you have spirit, do you? Well, it's more than I can say for that father of yours, too yellow and too drunk to carry out the Queen of Castile's bid—"

The hand flashed out again but this time the big man caught it in one of his own and twisted sideways against the girl, forcing her back against the table's edge. "I like my girls to struggle," he said, and the girl's face went white as she suddenly let herself go limp in his arms.

The man grinned. "Oh I like 'em limp, me lass. When they're pretty as a rose, like you, who's to care?"

"Papa!" the girl screamed. The big man's face hovered over hers, blotting out the oil-lamp lights, the thick lips all but slavering....

"Just a minute, man!" Danny cried, striding boldly to them. Hardly pausing in his efforts to kiss the again struggling girl, the big man swatted back with one enormous arm and sent Danny reeling. Whoever he was, he was a popular figure. The laughter was still louder now. Everyone was having a great time, at Danny's expense now.

Danny crashed into a chair, upending it. A bowl of soup came crashing down, the heavy bowl splintering, the hot contents scalding him. He stood up and heard the girl scream. Instinctively, he grasped two legs of the heavy chair and hefted it. Then he sprinted back across the room.

"Behind you, Pietro!" a voice cried, and at the last moment the big man whirled and faced Danny, then lunged to one side, taking the girl with him.

Danny couldn't check his arms, which had carried the heavy chair overhead. It came down with a crash against the edge of the big plank table. The chair shattered in Danny's arms. One leg flew up and struck the big man in the face, though, bringing blood just below the cheek bone. He bellowed in surprise and pain and came lumbering toward Danny.

Danny was aware of the girl cowering to one side, aware that another of the chair's legs was still grasped in his right hand. He was but a boy, he found himself thinking quickly, desperate. If the giant grabbed him, grabbed him just once, the fight would be over. The man was twice his size, twice his weight. Yet he had to do something to help the girl....

The giant came at him. The big arms lifted over the heavy, brutal face.... And Danny drove under them with the chair-leg, jabbing the tip of it against the man's enormous middle. Pietro—for such was the man's name—sagged a few inches, the breath rushing, heavy with garlic, from his mouth. But still, he got his great hands about Danny's throat and began to squeeze.

Danny saw the wood rafters, the window, a bargirl standing, mouth open, watching them, the drunken man and his daughter, then a blurry, watery confusion as his eyes went dim. He was conscious of swinging the club, of striking something, of extending the club out as far as it would go and then slamming it back toward himself, striking something which he hoped was Pietro's head. He felt his mouth going slack and wondered if his tongue were hanging out. Exerting all his strength he struck numbly, mechanically, desperately with the chair-leg.

And slowly, the constriction left his throat. Something struck against his middle, almost knocking him down. Something pushed against his legs, backing him against the table. He looked down. His eyes were watery, his throat burning. The giant Pietro lay, breathing stertorously, at his feet.

A small hand grabbed his. "Father will come now," a voice said. "I don't—don't even know who you are, but I want to thank you. I thank you for myself and the Queen, and God, senor. You better come quickly, with us. Does it hurt much?"

Danny tried to talk. His voice rasped in his throat. The girl squeezed his hand and together with her and the drunken man who was her father, he left the tavern. The giant Pietro was just getting up and shaking his fist at them slowly....

It was a small top-floor room in an old waterfront building in the Spanish port of Palos. Or, Danny corrected himself, the Castillian port of Palos. Because, in this year of our Lord 1492, Spain had barely become a unified country.

"Are you feeling better, Martin Pinzon?" the beautiful girl asked him.

He had given the name he had heard, Martin Pinzon, as his own. The room was very hot. The August night outside was hot too and sultry and starless. The girl's father was resting now, breathing unevenly. The girl's name was Nina. One of the small caravels in her father's three-ship fleet was named after her. Her full name was Nina Columbus.

Nina brought another wet cloth and covered Danny's swollen throat with it. "Does it hurt much?" she said, and, for the tenth time, "we have no money to thank you with, senor."

"Any man would have—"

"But you were the only one. The only—never mind. Martin, listen. I have no right to trouble you, but ... it's father. Tomorrow is the second day of August, you see, and it is all over Palos that tomorrow he sails with the Queen's charter...."

"Then if you're worrying about that big man, Pietro, you can forget it. If you're sailing, I mean."

"That's just it," Nina said desperately. "Father doesn't want to sail. Martin, tell me, do you believe the world is round?"

Danny nodded very soberly. "Yes, Nina," he told her softly. "The world is round. I believe it."

"My father doesn't! Funny, isn't it, Martin?" she said in a voice which told him she did not think it was funny at all. "All Spain—and Genoa too—think that tomorrow morning my father, Christopher Columbus, will journey to the unexplored west confident that he will arrive, after a long voyage, in the East—when really my father, this same Christopher Columbus, lies here in a drunken stupor because he lacks the courage to face his convictions and ... oh, Martin!" Her voice broke, her pretty face crumpled. She sobbed into her hands. Gently, Danny stroked her back.

"There now, take it easy," he said. "Your father will sail. I know he'll sail. Do you believe the world to be round, little Nina?"

"Yes. Oh yes, yes, yes!"

"He will sail. He will prove it and be famous. I know he will."

"Oh, Martin. You sound so sure of yourself. I wish I could ..."

"Nina, listen. Your father will sail."

"You'll help us you mean?"

"Yes. All right, I'll help you. Now, get some sleep if you want to wake up and say goodbye to him in the morning. Because I'll be getting him up before the sun to—"

"Are you a sailing man too? Are you going with him?"

"Well ..."

"Wait! Martin, I remember you now. Martin Pinzon. At the meeting of the organization to prove the Earth's round shape. You! You were there. And once, once when he was not drunk, father said that a Don Pinzon would command one of our three ships, the Nina it was, the caravel which bears my name. Are you this Don Pinzon?"

Slowly, Danny nodded. He remembered his history now. The Nina *had* been commanded by one Don Pinzon, Don Martin Pinzon! And he was now this Martin Pinzon, he, Danny Jones. Which meant he was going with Columbus to discover a new world! A nineteen-year-old American youth going to witness the single most important event in American history....

"Yes," Danny said slowly, "I am Don Pinzon."

"But—but you're so young!"

Danny shrugged. "I have seen more of the world than you would believe, Nina."

"The Western Sea? You have been out on the Western Sea, as far as the Canary Islands, perhaps?" she asked in an awed voice.

"I know the Western Sea," he said. "Trust me."

She came very close. She looked long in his eyes. "I trust you, Martin. Oh yes, I trust you. Listen, Martin. I'm going. I'm going with you. I have to go with you."

"But a girl—"

"He is my father. I love him, Martin. He needs me. Martin, don't try to stop me. I want you to help me aboard, to see that he ... oh, Martin, you'll have so much to do. Because the rest of our crew—some of them being hired even now by the three caravel pursers—will be a crew of cut-throats and ne'er-do-wells embarking into the unknown because they have utterly nothing to lose. Father needs you because the others won't care."

"The three caravels will sail west," Danny told her. "Believe me, they'll sail west. Now, get some sleep."

Her face was still very close. Her eyes filled with tears, but they were not tears of sadness. She took his cheeks in her hands and kissed him softly on the lips. She smiled at him, her own lips trembling.

"Martin," she said.

His arms moved. They went around her, drew the softness of her close. She murmured something, but he did not hear it. His lips found hers a second time, fiercely. His hands her shoulder, her throat, her ...

"Flat," Columbus mumbled. "Flat. Abs'lutely flat. The Earth is—flat as a pancake...."

"Oh, Martin!" Nina cried.

It was raining in the morning. A hard, driving rain, pelting down on the seaport of Palos. The three caravels floated side by side in the little harbor and a large, derisive crowd had gathered. The crowd erupted into noisy laughter when Columbus and his little party appeared on foot.

"I need a drink," Columbus whispered. "I can't go through with it."

"Father," Nina said. "We're with you. I'm here. Martin is here."

"I can't go—"

"You've got to go through with it! For yourself and for the world. Now, stand straight, father. They're looking at you. They're all looking at you."

Columbus, thought Danny. The intrepid voyager who had discovered a new world! He smiled grimly. Columbus, the history books should have said, the drunken sot who didn't even have the courage to face his own convictions.

They walked ahead through the ridiculing crowd. Danny's throat was still sore. He was not frightened, though. He possibly was the only man in the crew who was not frightened. The others didn't care what their destination was, true: but they wanted to reach it alive. Danny knew the journey would end in success. The end of the journey meant nothing to him. It was written in history. It was ...

Unless, he suddenly found himself thinking, I came back here to write it. He grinned at his own bravado. What would they have said in freshman psych— that was practically paranoid thinking. As if Danny Jones, Whitney College, Virginia, U.S.A., could have anything to do with the success or failure of Columbus' journey.

They reached the small skiff that would take them out to the tiny fleet of caravels. The crowd hooted and jeered.

"... going to drop off the edge of the world, Columbus."

"If the monsters don't get you first."

"Or the storms and whirlpools."

Columbus gripped Nina's hand. Martin-Danny took his other arm firmly and steered him toward the prow of the skiff. "Easy now, skipper," Danny said.

"I can't—"

"There's wine on the Santa Maria," Danny whispered. "Much wine—to make you forget. Come on!"

"And I'm going, father," Nina said. "Whether you go or not."

"You!" Columbus gasped. "A girl. You, going—"

"With Martin Pinzon. If—if my own father can't look after me, then Martin can."

"But you—" Danny began.

"Be quiet, please," she whispered as Columbus climbed stiffly into the skiff. "It may be the only way, Martin. He—he loves me. I guess I'm the only thing he cares about. If he knows I'm going."

"To the Santa Maria!" Columbus told the rowers as Danny and Nina got into the skiff.

"To the New World!" cried Danny melodramatically.

"What did you say?" Nina asked him.

His face colored. "I mean, to the Indies! To the Indies!"

The skiff bobbed out across the harbor toward the three waiting caravels. Departure time had arrived.

Two hours later, they were underway.

The sea was calm as glass, green as emerald. The three caravels, after a journey of several days, had reached the Canary Islands where additional provisions and fresh water were to be had.

"This," said Columbus, waving his arms to take in the chain of islands. "This is as far as a mere man has a right to go. There is nothing further, can't you see? Can't you?"

He was sober. Danny had come over in a skiff from the Nina to see that he remained sober at least for the loading and the departure. It was as if he, Danny, was going to preserve Columbus' name for history—single-handed if necessary.

"We will not go on," Columbus said. "We're going back. The only way to the Indies is around the Cape of Storms, around Africa. I tell you—"

"That's enough, father," Nina said. "We ..."

"I'm in command here," Columbus told them. It surprised Danny. Usually, the drunken sailor was not so self-assertive. Then it occurred to Danny that it wasn't merely self-assertiveness: it was fear.

Danny called over the mate, a one-legged man named Juan, who walked with a jaunty stride despite his peg leg. "You take orders from Columbus?" Danny said. "Would you take orders from me?"

Juan shook his head, smiling. "You command aboard the Nina only, Martin Pinzon. I heard what the Captain said. If he wants to go back and give up this fool scheme, it's all right with me. And you know the rest of the crew will say the same."

Nina looked at Danny hopelessly. She said, "Then, then it's no use?"

Danny whispered fiercely, "Your father loves you very much?"

"Yes, but—"

"And doesn't want to see anything happen to you?"

"But—"

"And believes the world is flat and if you sail far enough west you'll fall off?"

"But I—"

"Then you're coming with me aboard the Nina!"

Columbus gasped, "What did you say?"

"She's coming with me, on the Nina. If you don't want to find the western route to the Indies, we will. Right, Nina?" he said, taking her hand and moving to where the rope-ladder dangled over the side of the Santa Maria to the skiff below.

"Don't take her from this deck," Columbus ordered.

Danny ignored him. "Don Juan!" cried Columbus, and the peg-leg came toward Danny.

"I'm sorry, Don Martin," he said, "but—"

Still holding Nina's hand, Martin stiff-armed him out of the way and ran for the side. Someone jerked the rope-ladder out of reach and someone else leaped on Martin. For, he was Martin now, Martin Pinzon. His own identity seemed submerged far below the surface, as if somehow he could look on all this without risking anything. He knew that he was merely a defense mechanism, to ward off fear: for, it wasn't true. If Martin Pinzon were hurt, *he* would be hurt.

He hurled the man from his back. Nina screamed as a cutlass flashed in the sun. Martin-Danny ducked, felt the blade whizz by overhead.

"Jump!" Martin-Danny cried.

"But I can't swim!"

"I can. I'll save you." It was Danny again, completely Danny. He felt himself arise to the surface, submerging Martin Pinzon. Because the Spaniard probably couldn't swim at all, and if Danny made promises, it was Danny who must fulfill them.

He squeezed Nina's hand. He went up on the side—and over. The water seemed a very long way down. They hit it finally with a great splash.

Down they went and down, into the warm murky green depths. Down—and finally up. Danny's head broke surface. He was only yards from the skiff. He had never let go of Nina's hand, but now he did, getting a lifeguard's hold on her. He struck out for the skiff.

Fifteen minutes later, they were aboard the Nina. "I command here," Danny told the crew. "Is that correct?"

"Aye, sir," said Don Hernan, the mate.

"Even if Columbus tells you different?"

"Columbus?" spat Don Hernan. "That drunkard is in command of the Santa Maria, not the Nina. We follow Martin Pinzon here."

"Even if I give one set of orders and Columbus another?"

"Even then, my commander. Yes."

"Then we're sailing west," Danny cried. "Up anchor! Hurry."

"But I—" Nina began.

"Don't you see? He thinks I'm abducting you. Or he thinks I'm sailing west with you to certain death. He will follow with the Santa Maria and the Pinta, trying to rescue you. And we'll reach the Indies. Columbus will sail across the Western Sea to save his daughter, but what's the difference *why* he'll sail. The important thing is, Queen Isabella gave him the charter and the caravels and with them he's making history. You see?"

"I ... I think so," Nina said doubtfully.

A heady wind sprang up. The square-rigged sails billowed. The Nina began to surge forward—into the unknown West.

Tackle creaked aboard the nearby Santa Maria and Pinta. The two other caravels came in pursuit. But they won't catch us, Martin knew. They won't catch us until we reach—Hispaniola. And then, pursuit will be no more. Then, it will no longer matter and we'll all be heroes....

Which is the way it turned out—almost.

The Santa Maria and Pinta pursued all through August and September and into October, but the Nina kept its slim lead. The ships were never out of sight of one another and once or twice Columbus even hailed them, imploring them to return to Spain with him. When they ignored him, his deep voice boomed to his own crew and the crew of the Pinta: "Then sail on, sail on!" It was these words, Danny knew, that history would record. Not the others.

One morning in October, he awoke with a start. Something had disturbed his sleep—something ...

"Good morning, captain," a voice said.

He looked up. It was a giant of a man, with a hard face and brutal-looking eyes. He knew that face. Pietro! The giant of the tavern.

"But you—"

"I was aboard all the time, my captain," Pietro said. "An auxiliary rower. You never knew." He said nothing else. He lunged at Martin's bunk—for I'm Martin again, Danny thought—a knife gleaming in his big hand.

Martin-Danny sat up, bringing the covers with him, hurling them like a cloak at Pietro. The giant's knife-hand caught in the covers and Danny swung to his feet, shoving the big man. Pietro stumbled into the bunk, then lashed around quickly, unexpectedly, the knife loose again. Danny felt it grating across his ribs hotly, searingly. He staggered and almost fell, but somehow made it to the door and on deck. He needed room. Facing that knife in the close confines of the cabin, he was a dead man and knew it.

He hit the stairs and headed for the deck. He reached the door—tugged. It held fast. He heard Pietro's laughter, then threw himself to one side. The knife thudded into the wood alongside Danny's shoulder.

Then the door came open, throwing him back. He stumbled, regained his balance, plunged outside. With a roar, Pietro followed him, knife again in hand.

Danny backed away slowly. Only a few crew members were on deck now, and a watch high up in the crow's nest. The watch was crying in an almost-delirious voice: "Land, land! Land ho-oo!" But Martin-Danny hardly heard the words. Pietro came at him—

Suddenly Don Hernan was in front of him. Don Hernan's hand nipped up and then down and a knife arced toward Danny. He caught it by the haft, swung to face the giant. But, he thought, I don't know how to use a knife. I'm Danny Jones, I ...

Pietro leaped, the knife down, held loosely at his side, underhanded, ready to slash and rip. Danny sidestepped and Pietro went by in a rush. Danny waited.

Pietro came back carefully this time, crouching, balanced easily on the balls of his feet. For all his size, he fought with the grace of a dancer.

Danny felt warm wetness where the blood was seeping from his ribs. Feet pounded as more of the crew came on deck in response to the watch's delirious words. Instead of crowding at the prow, though, they formed a circle around Danny and Pietro. Danny thought: But I'm the captain. The captain. They ought to help me ... they ... He knew though that they would not. They were a fierce, proud people and the law of single combat would apply even to the captain who had piloted them across an unknown ocean.

Pietro came by, attempting to slash with his knife from outside. Danny moved quickly—not quick enough. The knife point caught his arm this time. He felt his hand go numb. His own knife clattered to the deck as blood oozed from his biceps.

Once more Pietro charged him. Weaponless, Danny waited. Pietro was laughing, sure of himself—

Careless.

Danny slipped aside as Pietro brought the knife around in a wicked swipe. He spun with it and when he came around Danny was waiting for him. He drove his left fist into the great belly and his right to the big, bearded jaw. Pietro slumped, disbelief in his eyes. He swung the knife again but only succeeded in wrapping his giant arm around Danny. He bent his head, shook it to clear it of the sting of Danny's blows. And Danny rabbit-punched him.

Pietro went down heavily and someone shouted. "The face! Kick him in the face!"

Wearily, Danny shook his head. He went with Nina to the rail and saw the green palm-fringed island of the New World. Nina smiled at him, then ripped something from what she was wearing and began to bandage his ribs, his arm.

They heard a splash. Danny looked around, saw Don Hernan and a member of the crew gazing serenely down. Pietro was down there, where they had tossed him. For a while the body floated, then the limbs splashed wildly as Pietro regained consciousness. He drifted back away from the ship. He went under, and came up. He went under again, and stayed under....

"The Indies," Nina said.

"The Indies," Danny said. He did not make the distinction between east and west. They must learn for themselves.

The Pinta and the Santa Maria came up alongside. All thoughts of pursuit were gone. Columbus waved. He was very close now on the deck of the Santa Maria. There was something in his face, something changed. Columbus was a new man now. He had been shamed. He had followed his daughter and Martin Pinzon across an unknown ocean and he was changed now. Somehow, Danny knew he could now make voyages on his own.

"Martin," Nina whispered. "They may say it was father. But it was you. I'll know in my heart, it was you."

Danny nodded. She put her arm around his shoulder, and kissed him. He liked this slim girl—he liked her immensely, and it wasn't right. She wasn't his, not really. She was Martin Pinzon's. He let the Spaniard come to the surface, willed his own mind back and down and away. She's all yours, Pinzon, he told the other mind in his body. She—and this world. I'm a— stranger here.

But once more he kissed Nina, fiercely, with passion and longing.

"Goodbye, my darling," he said.

"Goodbye! What—"

He let Martin Pinzon take it from there. "Hello," said Martin Pinzon. "I mean, hello forever, darling."

She laughed. "Goodbye to your bachelorhood, you mean."

"Yes," he said. "Yes."

But it was Martin Pinzon talking now. Completely Martin Pinzon.

He was back in his grand-uncle's basement. He was in the trunk and he felt stiff. Mostly, his right arm and the right ribs felt stiff. He felt his shirt. It was caked with blood.

Proof, he thought. If I needed proof. What happened to Pinzon happened to me.

He stood up. He felt weak, but knew he would be all right. He knew about Columbus now. At first, a weak drunkard. But after the first voyage, thanks to Martin Pinzon and Nina, an intrepid voyager. For history said Columbus would make four voyages to the New World—and four he would make.

Danny went outside, to where the lawyer was waiting for him. The trunk was Danny's now, the time trunk. And he would use it again, often. He knew that now, and it was wrong to deflate a dream.

Columbus was a hero. He would never say otherwise again.

THE END

Milton Keynes UK
Ingram Content Group UK Ltd.
UKHW012315040624
443649UK00007B/658

9 789361 470219